Owlbert

For a free color catalog describing Gareth Stevens' list of high-quality children's books call 1 (800) 433-0942

Library of Congress Cataloging-in-Publication Data

Harris, Nicholas, 1973-
      Owlbert / Nicholas Harris ; Karl Josef Horvat [illustrator].
            p. cm.
            Contents: Nicholas longs for a pet, but his parents say, "No," until
one with all the right qualifications comes along.
      ISBN 0-8368-0110-5
            [1. Owls--Fiction. 2. Children's writings.] I. Horvat, Karl Josef, ill.
      II. Title.
      PZ7.H24340w   1989
      [E]--dc19   89-4445

North American edition published in 1989 by

Gareth Stevens Children's Books
7317 West Green Tree Road
Milwaukee, Wisconsin, USA 53223

North American edition copyright © 1989
by Gareth Stevens, Inc. First published
in South Australia by Era Publications.
Text copyright © 1988 by Nicholas Harris.
Illustrations copyright © 1988 by Karl
Josef Horvat.

Printed in the United States of America

1 2 3 4 5 6 7 8 9 95 94 93 92 91 90 89

Owlbert

Written by Nicholas Harris
Illustrated by Karl Josef Horvat

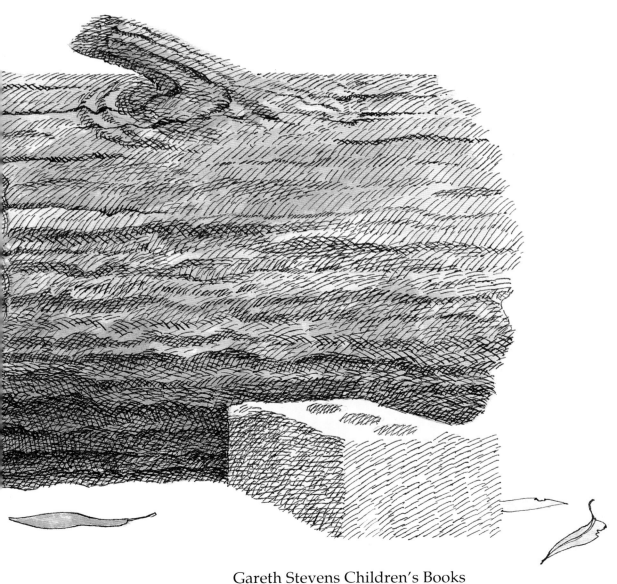

Gareth Stevens Children's Books
MILWAUKEE

Nicholas went to a pet shop and saw some beautiful birds.
He wanted a bird of his own.

"No," said his parents. "Birds drop seeds everywhere."

He borrowed two books about dogs from the local library.
"I'd love a pet dog," Nicholas told his father.

"No," said his father. "Dogs cost too much to feed."

"Mom," said Nicholas,
"my friend Rachel has twelve pet mice
she wants to give away. Can I have them?"

"No," said his mother. "Mice smell."

"Gee, I'll *never* have a pet," said Nicholas.

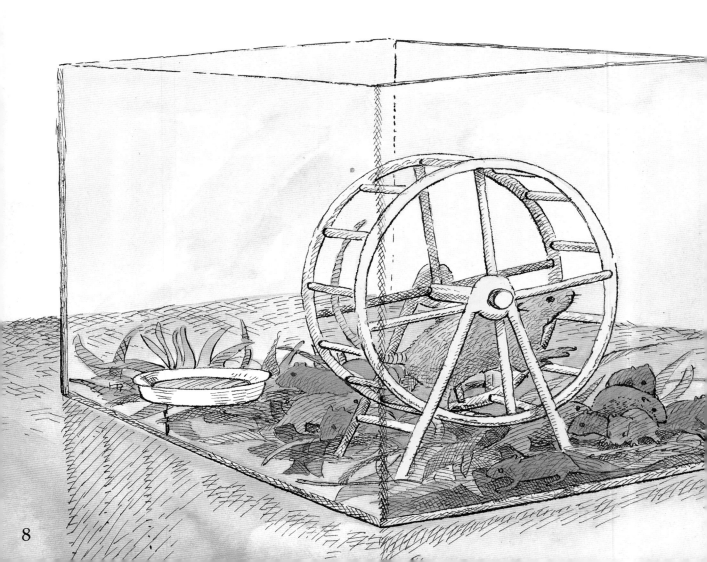

One day, Nicholas was climbing an old tree
when he found a dead owl.

While he was looking at it,
he heard a shrill, trilling whistle.

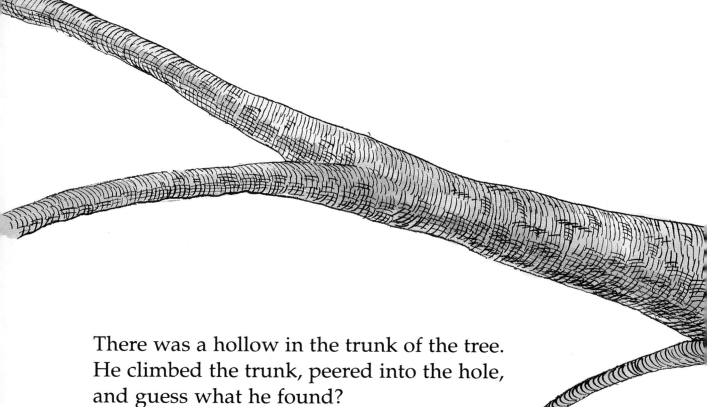

There was a hollow in the trunk of the tree.
He climbed the trunk, peered into the hole,
and guess what he found?

It was an owlet!
Nicholas knew by its feathers
that it was about four weeks old.
Without a parent, the baby owl would die!

The owlet blinked back at Nicholas
through its white-rimmed spectacles
and gave another faint whistle.

"It's hungry," thought Nicholas.

He picked it up and gently tucked it inside his pocket.
After a few wriggles and squirms, the owlet settled,
and Nicholas climbed carefully down the tree.

He tried to think of a place
to hide the owlet from his parents,
because he knew what they would say.

"The tree house!" Nicholas said to himself.
"They wouldn't get up there in a million years."

So the little owlet was placed
in a wooden crate in the tree house.

Feeding was going to be a problem.

Nicholas crept cautiously into the kitchen.
Some mincemeat was defrosting.
He took a piece and climbed to the tree house.

The owlet gobbled some mincemeat,
fluffed up its feathers, and fell asleep.

That night Nicholas was too excited to sleep.
"I'll call him *Owlbert*," he chuckled, "after my father."

He wondered what he was going to feed Owlbert.
Owlbert was wondering what he was going to eat.

Each day, Nicholas collected grasshoppers and other insects.
Each evening he fed some to his owl.
The rest he put in a plastic bag and stored for later.

Owlbert's appetite grew.
The more he ate, the bigger he grew,
until he was too big for his little crate.

So Nicholas found a hollow log for him.

He blocked one end to keep the wind out.
In the other end, he made a round door.

This would be Owlbert's new home . . .
at least, until he grew too big again.

So Nicholas cared for Owlbert,
and Owlbert adopted Nicholas as his "parent,"
and it was their secret.

Eventually it happened.
The time came for Owlbert to look after himself.
So one night, Nicholas left the log door open.
Later he climbed the tree to check.

Owlbert was not there.
"Will he come back?" he wondered.
It was a long night.

In the morning, he found Owlbert in his log again,
and decorating the tree-house platform
were the remains of a finished meal.

Nicholas had not lost him as a pet.
Owlbert was free—but still a friend.

One evening, Nicholas and his family
were having a barbecue.

Just as Nicholas was about to eat,
Owlbert swooped down next to him.

His parents were amazed
when the two friends shared a sausage.

"His name is Owlbert, he looks after himself,
and he lives outside," Nicholas explained quickly.

"Owlbert?" his father chuckled. "I like the name."
"He's amazing!" exclaimed his mother.

To *this* pet, they could not say "no."
So Owlbert became part of the family.